Before You

Rebecca Doughty

HOUGHTON MIFFLIN HARCOURT
Boston New York

I was a flower with no pot.

I was a polka with no dot.

I was a tail without a wag.

Just a bean without a bag.

I was a noodle without soup.

Just a cone without a scoop.

I was a bowl without a fish.

A birthday cake without a wish.

A tub without a rubber duck.

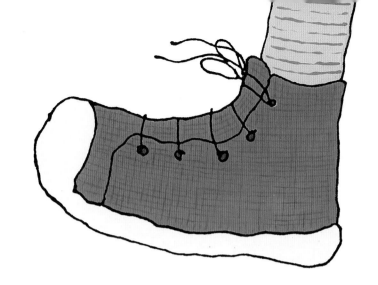

A four-leaf clover with no luck.

I was a sky without the blue.

I was a ME without a YOU.

Then you arrived and changed the tune!

You woke the sun.

You lit the moon.

You put the splash into the puddle.

You put the squeeze into the cuddle.

You put the fizz into the pop.

You put the flip into the flop.

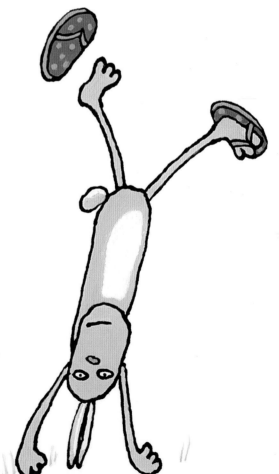

You put the cozy in the nook.

You put the story in the book.

I had a cup, you brought the tea.

I had a boat, you brought the sea.

I had a drum, you brought the beat.

I had a dream, you made it sweet.

Now I'm a bird and you're my song.

So tell me now...

...what took you so long?

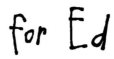

for Ed

www.hmhco.com

The text of this book is set in Garamond 3 LT Std.
The illustrations were created with ink and Flashe paint.

Library of Congress Cataloging-in-Publication Data
Doughty, Rebecca, 1955–
Before you / written by Rebecca Doughty.
pages cm
Summary: "Celebrates how the love of another can change one's life for the
better"— Provided by publisher.
ISBN 978-0-544-46317-2
[1. Stories in rhyme. 2. Love—Fiction.] I. Title.
PZ8.3.D743Bef 2016
[E]—dc23
2015018748

Manufactured in China
SCP 10 9 8 7 6 5 4 3 2 1
4500617830